Captain and Ladybird and Herbert watched as the tailgate was lowered. Then they shook their great heads in disgust as down it walked an old grey donkey.

"Good afternoon," she said. "My name is Jenny."

"It is not a good afternoon," said Captain.

"And as far as we are concerned," said Herbert, "your name is mud."

"You may not be aware," said Ladybird in his most patronizing of voices, "that this is a Home for horses."

"And not," said Captain, "for whatever sort of animal you may be."

"I think," said Herbert, blowing a snort of disgust through his large nostrils, "that it's an ass."

"Come away, boys," said Ladybird, "and leave the wretched creature. You don't know where it's been."

All three turned and walked majestically back to the shade of the sycamore tree . . .

HORSE PIE

DICK KING-SMITH

Horse Pie

Illustrated by Valerie Littlewood

YOUNG CORGI

HORSE PIE
A YOUNG CORGI BOOK : 0 552 55399 9

First published in Great Britain by Doubleday,
a division of Random House Children's Books

PRINTING HISTORY
Doubleday edition published 1993
Young Corgi edition published 1994

Set in Linotype Bembo by
Chippendale Type Ltd

Young Corgi Books are published by Random House Children's Books,
61–63 Uxbridge Road, London W5 5SA,
a division of The Random House Group Ltd,
in Australia by Random House Australia (Pty) Ltd,
20 Alfred Street, Milsons Point, Sydney, NSW 2061, Australia,
in New Zealand by Random House New Zealand Ltd,
18 Poland Road, Glenfield, Auckland 10, New Zealand
and in South Africa by Random House (Pty) Ltd,
Isle of Houghton, Corner of Boundary Road & Carse O'Gowrie,
Houghton 2198, South Africa.

Printed and bound in Great Britain by
Cox & Wyman Ltd, Reading, Berkshire.

CONTENTS

HORSE PIE

Chapter One

"She'll have to go," said the
donkeyman.

"Who?" said his son, Sam.

"Old Jenny. She's got so slow.
Didn't you see that kid just now
trying to make her walk a bit faster?
She was miles behind the others.
She's past it."

Sam squiggled sand between his

bare toes as he looked at the line of donkeys, waiting patiently for their next riders.

"What will happen to her, Dad?" he said.

"Have to see if they've got room for her at the Donkey Sanctuary," said his father.

"And if they haven't?"

"Cats' meat, I'm afraid," said the donkeyman.

"You mean . . .?"

"Yes. Have to send the old girl to the slaughterhouse."

"Oh, Dad, you couldn't! Not old Jenny!" Sam pleaded.

"Well, you think of a better idea then."

"Have a look at this," said the

Manager of the Old Horses' Home to his stableman, a couple of days later.

"What is it, boss?"

"Letter from a kid. Son of the chap that keeps the beach donkeys at Easton-super-Mare."

The stableman read the letter.

" '. . . Donkey Sanctuary full up . . . slaughterhouse . . . you are her last hope . . . Please, please!' Oh dear, pulls at your heart-strings, doesn't it, boss?"

The Manager nodded.

"He can't bear to think of her going to the knackers. We can make room for her, can't we?"

"Sure, boss," said the stableman. "What's one more among so many?"

And indeed there were a great many animals in the large, tree-shaded field in front of the Old Horses' Home. They were of all shapes and sizes, and all possible colours, and most of them were well past their prime. But amongst all the ancient ponies and horses were three giants who were, in fact, not old.

Captain and Ladybird were Shire horses, one black, one brown, and

both with white stockings. Herbert was a Suffolk Punch – a chestnut like all his kind. All three were in good health but there was no work for them to do – tractors had taken their places.

Far larger and heavier and stronger than the rest, Captain and Ladybird and Herbert looked down their great Roman noses at all the other horses in the place.

One afternoon, the three giants stood side by side under a sycamore tree, watching as a horsebox came up the drive.

"Another old crock, I suppose," said Captain.

"A broken-down nag, I expect," said Ladybird.

"Or a cow-hocked pony," said Herbert.

They moved with ponderous dignity towards the gate at the top corner of the field. Here the horsebox had stopped, and the stableman, who had come out to meet it, was opening the gate for it to reverse in.

Captain and Ladybird and Herbert watched as the tailgate was lowered. Then they shook their great heads in disgust as down it walked an old grey donkey.

"Good afternoon," she said. "My name is Jenny."

"It is not a good afternoon," said Captain.

"And as far as we are concerned," said Herbert, "your name is mud."

"You may not be aware," said Ladybird in the most patronizing of voices, "that this is a Home for horses."

"And not," said Captain, "for whatever sort of animal you may be."

"I think," said Herbert, blowing a snort of disgust through his large nostrils, "that it's an ass."

"Come away, boys," said Ladybird, "and leave the wretched creature. You don't know where it's been."

All three turned and walked majestically back to the shade of the sycamore tree.

Chapter Two

Jenny stood watching the three big horses sadly. She thought of all her friends left behind on the beach, and she stretched out her neck and gave a series of creaking, groaning heehaws – the loudest, most mournful noise imaginable.

Many of the other horses and ponies in the field looked up at this

sound, and one animal detached itself from the herd and came over to the donkey. It was a little old skewbald pony, bony and swaybacked, and it walked right up to Jenny and touched noses with her and said in a croaky voice, "Welcome."

"I don't think I am," Jenny said. "Those big horses were horrid to me."

"Don't take no notice," said the skewbald pony. "They'm like that, them three. My name's Alfie, by the way."

"I'm Jenny."

"Toffee-nosed lot they are," said Alfie, nodding his head towards the sycamore tree and the three huge rumps, one black, one brown, one chestnut, of Captain and Ladybird and Herbert. "And they're big-headed with it, not to mention the size of their backsides."

"They are rather fat," said Jenny.

"Fat as butter," said Alfie. "Just the job for the rustlers."

"What are they?"

"Horse-thieves. Chaps that do come round and nick horses."

"How do you know about these rustlers?" said Jenny.

"Heard tell about them from an old grey mare that used to live here. Dead now she is, but I can remember her telling me about these men that come round, at night usually, and steal livestock – cattle, sheep or horses. Once she saw a whole flock of sheep loaded

up into a lorry and driven away."

"But why would they want to steal those three big horses?"

"To ship 'em across the water. To France – it's not far. Be worth their while to come for those three great lumps of lard. Why, they must weigh nearly a tonne apiece," said Alfie.

"But what would they send them to France for?" asked Jenny.

"For meat," said Alfie. "Didn't you know they eat horses in France?"

Jenny let out another ear-shattering bray.

"Eat *horses*!" she said. "How dreadful!"

"Oh, I don't know," Alfie said. "After all, your Englishman eats

beef and lamb and pork. It's just
that he wouldn't think of eating
horses. He'd sooner keep 'em in a
Home like this, costing hundreds of
pounds to be looked after. But your
Frenchman, he's got more sense.
He sees a nice fat horse and he
thinks to himself, '*Ooh là là!* Horse-
pie!' "

"Do the French eat donkeys?"
Jenny said.

"I don't reckon so," Alfie said.
"They wouldn't eat you, old girl,
nor me, nor any of the old hat-racks
round here. We'm all skin and
bone. The rustlers wouldn't look at
us, so don't worry your head about
that."

But Jenny did worry. She was a
kindly animal by nature, and the

thought of the possible danger to Captain and Ladybird and Herbert upset her very much. Rude and overbearing they might be, but the idea of those magnificent creatures being stolen and taken away by lorry and then by ship to France, there to be killed and made into horse-pie – that was horrifying!

Chapter Three

For the rest of that day Jenny could think of nothing else as she grazed her way about the big field in Alfie's company.

Alfie, she noticed, though among the smallest of the ponies, was obviously a figure of some importance. He introduced her to the others as they met, and on the whole they greeted her in a friendly fashion. Though when a mare with a bit of breeding about her said, "An ass! What next?" she soon regretted it, for Alfie wheeled, quick as a cat, and his hind hooves beat a tattoo on her ribs.

But the three great carthorses were a different matter. One after another they worked their way close to the donkey and then, suddenly, lashed out or tried to bite her back. Once they lined up together and galloped across the field towards her, snorting and whinnying, as though they meant to squash her into the very ground.

"Let's hope the rustlers get you!" shouted Alfie as they dodged out of the way. "Horse-pie, that's all

you're good for!" But, of course, the thunder of hooves drowned his words.

"These rustlers," Jenny said. "When do they come?"

"At night," said Alfie. "Likely they'll have a big cattle-lorry parked down on the road, and then they'll come up the drive on foot, with halters."

"And how will they catch Captain and Ladybird and Herbert?"

"Sugar-lumps, I shouldn't wonder," said Alfie. "They'll go anywhere for a sugar-lump, they will. All the way to France, in fact."

"Alfie," said Jenny. "We must stop them."

"Stop who?"

"The rustlers."

"Whatever for, old girl? Good riddance to bad rubbish, I says. Nasty-tempered great things."

"I don't care about that," said Jenny. "They're still English horses and I'm an English donkey, and I'm not having them made into French horse-pies. We must stop the rustlers."

"Oh, nothing easier," said Alfie acidly. "You just waits by the gate and when the rustlers open it, you nips out and down the drive, and then you punctures all the tyres on the cattle-lorry."

"How do I do that?"

"Bite 'em."

For answer Jenny rolled back her lips, and Alfie could see that what

few teeth she had left were blunt
and brown and broken.

"Oh," he said. "Perhaps not."

"No," said Jenny, "but you've
given me an idea."

"What?"

" 'When the rustlers open the
gate,' you said."

"Well?"

"There's only one gate to this
field. There's no other way for
Captain and Ladybird and Herbert
to be taken out. The post-and-rail

fence is too high, even if they could be made to jump it."

"So?"

"We wait until the rustlers are in the field with their halters and their sugar-lumps, and then we block the gate."

"You're joking, old girl," said Alfie. "You and me, stood in the gateway, trying to stop the rustlers leading those three monsters through? We'd get killed."

"We might," said Jenny, "but we needn't be alone. All the other horses and ponies could help. The rustlers couldn't get through the whole herd."

The stableman, coming out to have a look round his horses, saw the

skewbald pony and the donkey
standing nose to nose. The pony
was nodding his head vigorously.

"You've got something there,
Jenny," Alfie said. "But they'd
drive us out of the way after a bit.
We shall need help from the
stableman. How're we going to get
him up in the middle of the night?"

"That's easy," Jenny said. "You
leave that bit to me."

Chapter Four

"It's a funny thing, boss," said the stableman to the Manager of the Home, some days later, "but those horses are acting ever so strange. Every evening at dusk they gather round the gateway, in a tight mass, and then after a bit they move away, but not too far away. It's almost as if they were practising something."

"All of them?" the Manager said. "They all do this?"

"Not Captain or Ladybird or Herbert," the stableman said. "They don't seem to be part of it."

"Beneath their dignity perhaps," the Manager said.

"I watched particularly last night," the stableman said, "and it's old Alfie and that donkey that seem to be the ringleaders. They go around from horse to horse, and then the whole lot move over to the gateway. It's since that donkey came."

"Funny," said the Manager, "but you've reminded me of something. There's talk of rustlers in the district."

"Taking horses?"

"Yes. For the French trade. Put a stout chain and padlock on that gate, will you? It's the only one into the field."

That evening, Jenny and Alfie watched as the stableman carried out his orders.

"That's all right then," Jenny said. "If the rustlers do come, they won't be able to get in."

"Be your age," said Alfie. "No, on second thoughts don't, you're old enough as it is. But they'll cut through that chain in a jiffy. They're professionals, these chaps, they know what to expect. Mark my words."

Alfie's words were marked a week later.

The evening parade of the herd around the gateway had just been dismissed, and only Alfie and Jenny still stood there in the dusk.

Suddenly Alfie put his muzzle against Jenny's long, hair-filled ear. "Look," he said softly.

They watched as a shadowy figure came walking up the drive. The man, they could see as he neared them, looked quite respectable – just an ordinary chap taking an evening stroll.

He stopped at the gate and leaned upon it, and looked about the darkening field. There was just enough light left to show, in their usual place beneath the sycamore, the three giant shapes.

"Watch," said Alfie as the man, after looking carefully around, put out a hand to examine the chain and padlock. Then he turned and went silently back.

"A rustler?" Jenny said.

"Looks like it. Haven't heard no lorry yet, it's too early."

"Shall we tell the others?" said Jenny. "We could always block the gateway to stop them getting in."

"No, no," said Alfie. "We wants them to come in and then we'll stop them getting out. Catch 'em red-handed. You go on down to the bottom by the road, old girl, and listen out for a lorry. Your ears are bigger than mine."

Chapter Five

Jenny was dozing by the rails when,
around midnight, she heard a
cattle-lorry approaching. It parked
just outside the fence, on the grass
verge of the road. Its lights were
switched off and three men got out
and very quietly lowered the
tailboard.

Jenny made off up the field.

"Look at that old moke!" one of the men said. "She's a walking skeleton."

"Don't think we'll bother with her," said a second man.

"Wait till you see the heavy horses," the third man said. "Why, they must weigh nearly a tonne apiece. Come on now, let's get a move on. I've got the bolt-cutters."

It was a darkish night, and the rustlers did not notice that, by the time they reached the gate, all the horses and ponies were alert, watching. The bolt-cutters made short work of the chain, and the men opened the gate, came into the field, closed the gate again, and set off towards the sycamore tree with their halters and their sugar-lumps. Behind them, the herd closed silently in front of the gateway.

Minutes passed, and then the

horses saw the three rustlers making their way back towards the gate. Behind each man walked a giant haltered shape, mumbling a sugar-lump.

"Right," said Alfie. "Stand firm, everybody." At his words, the ancients closed ranks even more tightly. Some faced the enemy, their yellow old teeth ready to bite. Some turned tail, prepared to kick the living daylights out of the rustlers. All stood waiting, dogged and determined.

"Get out of the way," the rustlers called, as quietly as they could. "Get out of it, you pack of miserable old deadbeats."

No-one moved.

Then Alfie's shrill neigh rang out.

"Captain! Ladybird! Herbert!" he cried. "Run for it! They're taking you to France, to make you into horse-pie!" At his words the three whirled away, dragging the halter-ropes from the men's hands, and thundered off across the field.

"Now, Jenny!" called Alfie, and from inside the donkey's aged frame came those awful creaking, groaning heehaws, loud enough to wake the dead.

The stableman woke with a start.
"Listen!" he said to his wife.
"The old donkey's braying, in the
middle of the night. That's not

natural. Something's wrong. Dial nine-nine-nine for the police. I'll get my gun," and he jumped out of bed.

Out in the field, the rustlers stood undecided, swearing, but Alfie had not done with them yet.

"Charge!" he cried, and now the whole herd of horses set off, straight at the rustlers, who threw themselves wildly over the fence and ran madly down the drive, pursued by the stableman. On the road a police car drew up beside the cattle-lorry.

Chapter Six

Down on the beach at Easton-super-Mare, the donkeyman leaned against one of his charges, reading the local newspaper. Suddenly he called to his son.

"Hey, Sam!" he cried. "Look at this!"

DONKEY FOILS RUSTLERS —
DRAMA AT OLD HORSES' HOME
A warning from an old donkey
led to the arrest of three horse-
thieves who were attempting to
steal stock from the Old Horses'
Home. As luck would have it,
the donkey chanced to bray loudly
in the middle of the night and
thus give the alarm. The police were
able to intercept the rustlers, who
will appear before local magistrates
next week.

"That's got to be our old Jenny, Dad!" said Sam. "It must be. She's the only donkey in the place."

"Wonder how she knew they were rustlers," said the donkeyman. "What a funny thing."

"Funny thing," said the Manager of the Old Horses' Home to the stableman as they stood by the gate, a couple of days later. "The two Shires and the Suffolk Punch seem to have taken quite a fancy to that old donkey. They never went near her before except to rough her up."

"I know," said the stableman. "Look at them all now, boss, standing together under the sycamore tree, chummy as can be. It's almost as though they realized

that they owe their lives to her. But of course they couldn't possibly know that."

Just then they heard a snickering beside them, and turned to see the old skewbald pony, baring his yellow teeth in what looked like a grin.

"Hello, Alfie," said the stableman. "What are you laughing at?"

THE END

ABOUT THE AUTHOR

Dick King-Smith was born in 1922 in Bitton, Gloucestershire. He is father, grandfather and great-grandfather to his ever-extending family and he likes nothing better than to surround himself with them.

Dick was a soldier, serving as a Lieutenant in the Grenadier Guards during World War II from 1941-1946. He then enjoyed a twenty-year career as a farmer, going on to try his luck at being a salesman, a factory worker and eventually a primary-school teacher, before hitting on the one thing he truly loved to do – tell stories. Dick now devotes his time to writing and has become one of the top ten best-selling children's authors in the UK.

All kinds of animals have played important roles in Dick King-Smith's life, especially pigs, for which he has a great fondness. His book *The Sheep-Pig* won the Guardian Award in 1984, and was later made into the irresistible motion picture, *Babe*.

When asked what he likes best about being a children's author, Dick replies, "Getting thousands of letters from children (and adults) all over the world, saying they've enjoyed what I do."

Dick's favourite place is his seventeenth-century cottage near Bristol – located only 3 miles from his birthplace. He writes all of his books in a small study, from where he's able to look out of the window at the countryside and retreat into his special world of fantasy, skilfully placing words into the mouths of the animal characters that he knows and loves so well.

THE GUARD DOG

Dick King-Smith

'Out of his hairy little mouth came the most awful noise you can possibly imagine . . .'

There are six puppies in the pet shop window; five posh pedigree puppies, and a scruffy little mongrel with a grand ambition – to be a guard dog.

The other pups laugh at him. How can such a small, scruffy dog possibly expect to be bought to guard a home? Especially when his bark is the most horrible, earsplitting racket they have ever heard! Will the poor little guard dog be doomed to a lonely life in the Dogs' Home – or worse . . .?

0 552 52731 9

YOUNG CORGI